IZZY

IN THE DOGHOUSE

Many of the designations used by manufacturers and sellers to distinguish their
products are claimed as trademarks. Where those designations appear in this book
and Kids Can Press Ltd. was aware of a trademark claim, the designations have been
printed in initial capital letters (e.g., Band-Aids).

Kids Can Press gratefully acknowledges the financial support of the Government
of Ontario, through Ontario Creates; the Ontario Arts Council; the Canada Council
for the Arts; and the Government of Canada for our publishing activity.

Published in Canada and the U.S. by Kids Can Press Ltd.
25 Dockside Drive, Toronto, ON M5A 0B5

Kids Can Press is a Corus Entertainment Inc. company

www.kidscanpress.com

The artwork in this book was created digitally.
The text is set in Arno Pro.

Edited by Yasemin Uçar
Designed by Andrew Dupuis

Printed and bound in Shenzhen, China, in 3/2020 by C & C Offset

CM 20 0 9 8 7 6 5 4 3 2 1

Library and Archives Canada Cataloguing in Publication

Title: Izzy in the doghouse / written by Caroline Adderson ; illustrated by Kelly Collier.
Names: Adderson, Caroline, 1963– author. | Collier, Kelly, illustrator.
Description: Series statement: Izzy ; 1
Identifiers: Canadiana 20190208139 | ISBN 9781771387323 (hardcover)
Classification: LCC PS8629.L46 H63 2020 | DDC jC813/.54 — dc23

IZZy
IN THE DOGHOUSE

Written by **Caroline Adderson**
Illustrated by **Kelly Collier**

Kids Can Press

CONTENTS

YUM.
A DIRT SANDWICH.

Isabel and Zoë were each other's favorite
friend — most of the time. They were so
much each other's favorite friend — most of
the time — that they had begged for side-
by-side cubbies at school. That way Isabel
could tuck her coat sleeve into Zoë's pocket
and Zoë could tuck her sleeve into Isabel's
pocket. Their coats were friends, too!

They made friendship bracelets for each
other and never took them off. The one
Isabel made for Zoë was pink and purple,

Zoë's favorite colors. Isabel's was red and yellow, fire truck colors, her favorites. At least the bracelets *started out* as pink and purple and red and yellow. After a month, the matted yarn looked more like different shades of gray and beige.

Today Isabel and Zoë were sitting side by side in the lunchroom wearing their gray-and-beige bracelets. Zoë pulled her sandwich out of her bag and made a face. "Yuck!"

"What?" Isabel asked.

"Seeds!" Zoë said.

She meant in the bread. Zoë didn't like bread with seeds because the seeds looked like dirt.

Last week, Isabel's nanny had packed a pickle in the same container as her sandwich and the bread got the mushes from the pickle juice. Isabel didn't like mushy food. Zoë had traded sandwiches with her then, so Isabel offered to trade now.

Isabel took a big bite of Zoë's sandwich. It was cheese, but she said, "Yum. A dirt sandwich."

Both girls started laughing so hard they couldn't eat at all.

This happened a lot. First, they would trade sandwiches, then Isabel would be eating dirt. Or they'd be reading quietly in the book nook, then they'd be doing gymnastics on the pillows. Or they'd be sitting in side-by-side cubicles in the bathroom whispering about lizards in the toilet, then they *were* lizards escaping the toilet, racing down the hall with toilet-paper tails streaming from the backs of their pants. They had a very big amount of fun together — most of the time.

The lunch monitor came over because they were laughing so loudly. "More chewing and swallowing from you two, please," she told them.

Zoë didn't like getting in trouble. She stopped laughing, so Isabel did, too. Lunch was a smaller amount of fun then.

After lunch, they went outside to play. "How about we make more dirt food?" Isabel said.

"Ha ha ha!" Zoë laughed.

They ran off to find some dirt. Easy! It was everywhere. They dug some out of the ground and shaped it into pies.

"We need more ingredients," Zoë said.

They stirred in some sand and crumbled pine cones, then reshaped the pies.

"So who's going to eat it?" asked Zoë, who didn't even like seeds.

Isabel smiled her biggest no-front-teeth smile. She poked her tongue in and out of the no-teeth space. Zoë hated when Isabel did that. Hated *and* loved it because then she could scream, "Yuck!!!"

After Zoë screamed about Isabel's tongue, Isabel stuck it out all the way and bowed tongue-first over the dirt pie.

"Izzy, don't *really* eat it!"

The closer Isabel's tongue got to the pie, the louder Zoë screeched.

Isabel touched the tip of her tongue to the dirt.

"YUCK!!!" Zoë screamed.

Actually, the dirt didn't taste like anything.

They were both laughing their heads off again when Bernadette and Nima came along. Isabel asked them, "Would you like to try some dirt?"

They hurried away.

"How about a pine cone?" Isabel called after them.

Then, still laughing, Isabel and Zoë put a few pine cones in their pockets and went looking for people to feed them to.

At the front of the school, they found two kindergarten boys piling up rocks. Isabel got an idea.

"Hey, do you want to play babies?" she asked them.

"No," answered one whose shoes were on the wrong feet.

Isabel said, "Come on. It's fun. We'll be your mothers and you'll be our babies. We'll feed you and love you."

"Feed us what?" the boy asked.

"Cookies," she said, because if she said pine cones, they wouldn't play. She patted her pockets so that Zoë would know what kind of cookies she meant. Zoë smiled. Both babies said yes.

Isabel and Zoë found a spot under a tree to be the nursery. "Which baby do you want?" Zoë asked.

Isabel picked the one with his shoes on the wrong feet. They hauled their babies into their laps. Right away, the babies began to wail. "Wa-wa-wa! We're hungry!"

The girls took the pine cones from their pockets and held them in front of their babies' faces.

"That's not a cookie," Isabel's baby said.

"Pretend it is," she told him.

Zoë's baby pretended, but Isabel's made a

tight line with his mouth and turned his head away.

"Coochie-coo," Isabel said, tickling him under the chin.

"Stop it," he said, wriggling in her arms.

Isabel let him go, but he got to his feet and started to *wa-wa-wa* again. For real this time! The playground monitor was standing nearby chatting with one of the teachers. When she heard the racket, she hurried over. Isabel's baby threw himself at the playground monitor and said, "She made me eat a pine cone!"

The playground monitor put both hands on her hips and frowned. "Girls? I think you know where you're going." She pointed to the school.

To the principal's office!

"Sorry," Isabel whispered to Zoë, but Zoë wouldn't look at her.

IN THE DOGHOUSE

Some of the time, Isabel and Zoë *weren't* each other's favorite friends. Because *some of the time*, the fun things they did ended in a no-fun way. Like when Zoë hit her head on the bookshelf in the book nook, or when they were sent to the principal's office for being lizards with toilet-paper tails ... or today, when they played babies with the kindergarten kids. Zoë hated getting sent to the principal's office.

The *some of the times* were hard for Isabel because Zoë was still *her* favorite friend. But

Isabel wasn't Zoë's. Even though they were both still wearing their matted gray-and-beige friendship bracelets, and their coat sleeves were still in each other's pockets, when Isabel rushed over to invite Zoë for a play date after school, Zoë made a teeny, pinched up, "I'm mad at you" mouth. Her mouth was so teeny that the words barely managed to squeeze out.

"I'm going to Bernadette's."

Bernadette was standing there, too, also making a teeny mouth even though Isabel hadn't got *her* in trouble. They walked away, holding hands like they were each other's favorite friend now and Isabel was nobody's.

Outside, Rosa, Isabel's nanny, was waiting to walk her home. As soon as Isabel saw her, she remembered Rosa's afternoon TV show. Isabel would have to sit there all alone waiting for it to finish, feeling even more like nobody's favorite friend. She looked around for someone else to invite. Patty!

Patty had piano lessons.

Nima came out next, but she had soccer.

Rosa said, "Izzy, let's go."

"I'll ask Ori. He likes my remote-control car."

"It's broken, remember? Let's go. My show's starting soon."

Isabel went, dragging her feet. It was how she walked, *some of the time*, when she wasn't Zoë's favorite friend.

Halfway across the schoolyard, Rosa said, "You'll ruin your shoes if you drag them like that, Izzy."

"I have lots of shoes," she said.

"That's no reason to ruin something. Lots of kids don't have any shoes at all."

Isabel perked up. "Can we invite them for a play date?"

"Did something happen today that nobody wants to play with you?" Rosa asked.

"No," Isabel said.

"Sometimes you're too bossy, Izzy."

"I'm not!"

"Okay."

"I'm not! I make *suggestions*."

"And did you suggest something today?"

In one huge breath, Isabel told Rosa. "I ate Zoë's dirt sandwich and then I ate some real dirt but nobody else would so we went around with pine cones and found some babies except mine wouldn't play properly because he was a real baby going wa-wa-wa."

"Izzy, can you speak slower?" Rosa said. "I'm confused."

Isabel thought of something then. "Did Mom come home from her trip yet?"

"Not yet."

"Can we go to the fire hall?"

"My show starts in ten minutes."

"Just for five minutes. Please. I want to say hi. I haven't been for so long."

"We went last week."

"Pleeeeeeeeeeeeeeeease!" Isabel said.

Rosa sighed. They turned down the fire hall street.

When they got there, the trucks were gone. Isabel rang the doorbell anyway, but nobody answered. There must have been a fire. That,

or the firefighters didn't want to be friends
with her anymore either.

"Maybe somebody's house caught fire,"
Isabel said as they headed for home.

"Maybe," Rosa said.

"Maybe it was Bernadette's house."

Rosa said nothing.

"Maybe we should check. Just go over and
see if there's smoke pouring out the windows.
And if there isn't, I'll just ring the doorbell
and say hi. I'll ask them to make sure that
the stove isn't on. They won't notice if it is,
because they're two girls having so much fun
without me."

"I think they'd smell the smoke."

"They might not. Then they'll be so

happy that I just happened to stop by and save their lives that they'll invite me in, even though Zoë's mad about getting sent to the principal's office."

"Ah," Rosa said. "So you and Zoë saw the principal today? And now you're in the doghouse?"

"Huh?" Isabel said. "What does that mean?"

Rosa put her arm around Isabel's shoulder again. "It means that Zoë's annoyed with you." Zoë was annoyed. She didn't want to play with Isabel.

"Give her a day or two," Rosa said. "She'll get over it. She always does."

When they got home, Rosa suggested that Isabel work on a craft. "Make some more of those friendship bracelets while I watch my show."

Isabel thought of something then. What if Zoë took off the pink-and-purple bracelet Isabel made for her? Then she noticed Rosa's arms.

"Rosa! You aren't wearing the bracelet I made for you. Aren't we friends anymore?"

"Of course we're friends, Izzy. That bracelet is precious to me. I put it away. I don't want it to get dirty like yours."

Rosa set down carrot sticks. Isabel crunched through one. She thought of Mom away on her business trip. "Is Mom wearing my bracelet?"

"I bet she is," Rosa answered.

"Can I phone and ask her?"

Rosa looked at the clock. "I don't think she'll be able to answer. Let me get the scissors and cut that bracelet off. You can make a pretty new one."

"No!" Isabel said, clutching the dirty, matted gray-and-beige bracelet to her chest. "Zoë made this for me. If I take it off, she'll think she's not my favorite friend anymore. But she is."

Rosa said, "I'll get the craft box just in case you change your mind and want to wear a pretty new one."

"Then I'd only be friends with myself!" Isabel called after her.

Rosa brought Isabel's craft box to the table anyway. Then she went to the living room to watch her show, closing the door behind her.

At school, there were so many NOs. NO talking at reading time. NO somersaulting in the book nook. NO writing backward. NO running in the hall. NO running backward in the hall. NO going into the boy's bathroom, even if nobody's there. NO making toilet-paper tails and running down the hall. NO showing your fire truck underwear to anybody *ever* — even if it's new. NO laughing instead of chewing and swallowing in the lunchroom. NO playing babies with the little kids.

Those were just this year's NOs — *so far.* And were the NOs written on a sign? NO. Were they written in a book? NO!

To find out what the NOs were, you had to go to Mrs. Kinoshita's office. Then Mrs. Kinoshita would personally tell you, "NO." She was nice. She never got mad. She just explained the NO.

And then you knew.

Home was easier. At home, Isabel knew all the NOs. The home NOs weren't written on a sign or in a book either, but Isabel knew them by heart because there were only two.

1. NO BARGING INTO THE BATHROOM WITHOUT KNOCKING!
2. NO BOTHERING ROSA WHILE SHE'S WATCHING HER SHOW!

But there was no NO about opening and closing the craft box thirty-two times, then going to check if the show was almost over. As long as you didn't ask out loud.

Isabel put her head in the door.

"It just started," Rosa said.

There was no NO about standing in the doorway to watch the show either, as long as you didn't ask what was happening, and what this or that Spanish word meant, and why the man with the mustache kissed so many different women ...

DOES IT TICKLE WHEN SOMEONE WITH A MUSTACHE KISSES YOU?

WOULDN'T IT MAKE YOU SNEEZE?

... as long as when Rosa asked you to please leave, you went.

"I'm going, I'm going!" Isabel said.

She went back to the table and finished her carrots while flipping the craft box lid open and closed.

There was no NO about peeking in again a little later. No NO about seeing Rosa crying her eyes out and running over and throwing yourself at her feet.

"I'm sorry, Rosa! I'm sorry I bothered you while you were watching your show!"

Rosa lifted Isabel off the floor. "Izzy, it's not you. It's the show. He doesn't love her anymore."

"Rosa? That's exactly what happened to me at school!!!"

GOTCHA!

Isabel lay in bed that night poking her tongue in and out of the no-teeth space in her mouth. Then she remembered that Zoë didn't like how it looked. What *did* it look like? Isabel wondered.

She got up, went to the bathroom and stood on the white plastic stool so she could see in the mirror.

Wow! She had so many freckles. She'd forgotten about them.

She stuck her tongue in the no-teeth space. It looked like a little pink worm poking its head out of a hole. *Cute*, Isabel thought.

She decided to get another opinion.

Rosa was in the downstairs bathroom.
Isabel knocked, but Rosa didn't answer.
Isabel pressed her ear to the door and heard
the shower running.

Inside the bathroom was like the inside of
a cloud. Isabel climbed up on the edge of the
sink and wiped a circle in the steam on the

mirror. Rosa was singing her favorite song about the *paloma* flying home. A *paloma* is a dove. "La la la, *paloma paloma!*" Isabel sang along. She stopped to poke her tongue in and out of the hole. "La la la, *paloma paloma!*" Poke, poke, poke.

Isabel didn't notice that the water had shut off, not until Rosa spoke from inside the shower. "Izzy? Remember our rule about privacy?"

"I knocked. You didn't answer. I just want to show you the worm in my mouth."

"What?!" Rosa stuck her face out from behind the shower curtain. She looked different wet.

"See?" Isabel showed her.

Rosa sighed. "Izzy, go back to bed."

"You look really different wet. Your hair's not curly anymore."

"Bed."

Isabel jumped down from the sink. "Good night, Rosa." She backed out of the room blowing kisses. "I love you, Rosa." She closed the door behind her.

Then she opened it again. Rosa shrieked and covered herself with the towel.

"I just wanted to tell you one more time that I love you," Isabel told her.

"Out!"

Isabel went to the living room and brought back some cushions, which she arranged on the floor outside the bathroom. She lay there listening to Rosa's beautiful *paloma* song

and the hair dryer going on, then off, and her beautiful tooth-brushing sounds … and then the not-beautiful sound of the squawk that Rosa made coming out of the bathroom and nearly stepping on Isabel.

"I just wanted to make sure you aren't mad at me," Isabel told her. "I won't be able to get to sleep if you are."

Rosa crouched down in her nightgown and gave Isabel a hug. "I'm not mad. I love you, Izzy. And Zoë loves you, too."

"Zoë's mad at me."

"Just a little bit. It doesn't mean she doesn't love you."

Rosa's flowery shampoo smell almost made Isabel gag, but her hug felt so good.

"Look," Isabel said. "The fire trucks on my pajamas are watering the flowers on your nightgown."

Rosa laughed.

"And the worm who lives in my mouth loves you, too. Look."

Poke, poke, poke.

Rosa put her hand over Isabel's mouth and whispered in her ear. "I'm going to tell you a secret. Then maybe you won't feel bad about Zoë. Maybe you'll be able to fall asleep."

"What?" Isabel asked. "What? What? What?"

"Your mom's coming home tonight. Late. She wanted to surprise you in the morning. Will you act surprised in the morning?"

"YES!!!" Isabel screamed, making Rosa jump about three feet in the air.

But Rosa was wrong. The secret about Mom coming home from her business trip didn't help Isabel fall asleep. The opposite! She was too excited to sleep.

She decided to stay up and surprise Mom before Mom could surprise her. When she heard Mom tiptoeing in, she was going to sit up in bed and shout, "Gotcha!"

She practiced until Rosa called up the stairs, "Izzy, you won't fall asleep if you're shouting!"

So she had to whisper the gotchas, which wouldn't surprise anybody.

But later, when Isabel tiptoed down to Rosa's room to ask if she was sure it was tonight because she'd been waiting so long and Mom still hadn't come, and she crept up beside Rosa and whispered, "Rosa?" Rosa shrieked and sat up.

So maybe a whisper was surprising.

"Are you sure it's tonight?" Isabel asked. "I've been waiting and waiting."

"Back to bed," Rosa said.

Isabel went. For a long time, she lay listening for the taxi. Then she got up and watched out the window. Then she went back to bed and listened hard again.

SIGH

Back and forth, back and forth. All the exercise was making her too tired to stay up and surprise Mom.

She went downstairs to check the clock: 11:42! She gathered the living room cushions and arranged them in the front hall. Then she curled up there, listening for the beautiful sound of the taxi pulling up.

The next thing she knew, she was in her own bed and Mom was giving her a kiss. Sleepily, Isabel said, "Gotcha …"

What a beautiful dream!

She sat up. She *was* in her own bed. That meant Mom was home!

Isabel tore downstairs and threw herself onto Mom's bed. "Gotcha, gotcha, gotcha!"

INCOMING!

GOTCHA!

"Ooof," Mom said.

Isabel reached for Mom's arm under the covers and felt the yarn around her wrist. "You *are* wearing my bracelet!" she cried.

"Of course I am, Izzy. I always wear it when I go away. It makes me feel close to you."

She let Isabel stay in her warm bed.

"Can you tell me the story?" Isabel asked.

"Now?" Mom said sleepily.

"Please?" Isabel said.

ONCE UPON A TIME

"Once upon a time, there was a woman who wanted a baby so badly ..." Mom began.

"That was you!" Isabel said.

"That's right." Mom yawned. "She waited and waited and no baby came into her life, so she decided one day to go to an agency. At the agency, she had to answer questions and fill out forms. Finally, after about a thousand questions and a thousand forms, the big rubber stamp came down."

"Tell me again what it said."

"Accepted."

"Accepted!" Isabel shivered all over with happiness. "I love that word! And then what happened?"

"I had to wait again. And wait and wait and wait."

"Like me tonight, waiting for you to come home."

"Only longer. Two years."

"Where was I?"

"You weren't born yet. That's what I was waiting for."

Not born yet! She snuggled into Mom. "Tell me about the phone call."

"One day, while I was at work, the phone rang. My desk phone, not the cell phone. I answered and a woman said, 'Is this Sheila?'"

I said, 'Yes. Who's this?' 'Someone with some very good news,' she said."

"It was me!" Isabel said. "Me! I was the good news! I got born!"

"When she said 'good news,' I began to shake all over. I could hardly hold the phone. I said, 'Is this about —' 'Yes,' she said. 'We have your —'"

"BABY!!!"

"At least that's what I thought she said, but I couldn't actually hear her because at that very moment —"

"THE FIRE ALARM WENT OFF! The woman on the phone was shouting to you BABY, BABY, BABY! And you were shouting back WHAT? WHAT? WHAT?"

"Shhh. You'll wake up Rosa."

Isabel whispered. "Everybody in the office left and you were still on the phone, right?"

"Right. Everybody had filed out just like we'd practiced in the fire drill."

"And then," Isabel said, "somebody noticed you weren't there."

Mom laughed. "That's exactly what happened."

"So the firefighters went to look for you. They went in every office. Finally, they found you on the phone, saying, 'WHAT? WHAT? WHAT?' Tell me what they said."

Mom put on her firefighter voice. "Ma'am, we are evacuating the building."

"And you told them, 'No! This is the

most important phone call of my life!'"

"Right."

"And then what happened?" Isabel held her breath. This was her most favorite part of the story.

Mom said, "They picked me up and carried me out."

HELLO? ARE YOU STILL THERE? HELLO? HELLO?

TOO MUCH LOVE

Whenever Mom returned from a business trip, they always played hooky the next day. Hooky was lying around in your pajamas watching movies and eating cheese puffs.

So it was too bad that the next morning everybody was grumpy from Not Enough Sleep. Rosa poured her coffee and took it to her room instead of eating breakfast with them like she usually did.

Mom said Isabel should try not to talk so loudly and so much this morning because the adults had headaches.

BLOOP

Actually, Isabel had a headache, too.
And she didn't feel like talking anyway. She
poured a small amount of cereal in her bowl
and a small amount of milk and ate it fast.
She did this four times. That way, the cereal
didn't get the mushes. The crunching hurt
the inside of her head, but it was better than
the mushes.

The best thing about hooky today was that Isabel wouldn't have to be nobody's favorite friend at school. When she went back tomorrow, Zoë wouldn't be mad anymore. She was never mad two days in row because after just one day, she started to miss Isabel as much as Isabel missed her.

Mom got on the phone and started talking about office things. Isabel tapped her on the shoulder to let her know she was waiting for hooky to start.

Mom covered the phone and said to Isabel, "Run and get dressed."

"Why?" Isabel asked.

Mom got up from the table and left the kitchen, which was when Isabel noticed she was wearing her work clothes, not her hooky pajamas.

Isabel followed her out. "Mom?"

She found Mom in the living room still saying office things. Isabel pulled on the arm that was wearing her friendship bracelet. "Mom?"

Mom smiled and lifted one finger in the air. *Wait a minute,* the finger was saying. Then she turned her back.

Isabel went around to stand in front of her, but Mom just turned her back again so she could concentrate on her office talk. Soon, they were turning in circles in the living room. Isabel started to feel dizzy.

Finally, Mom got off the phone. With a sad face, she told Isabel, "Izzy, honey? I'm so sorry. I really can't stay home today."

Mom had never canceled hooky before. Hooky was the only reason Isabel could stand it when Mom went away.

"But I can't go to school today," Isabel said. "I'm in the doghouse."

"I know you're disappointed, but I promise that tomorrow —"

Isabel flopped down on the sofa and burst into tears.

Mom sat beside her. "Izzy, I'm sorry."

Isabel kept on crying. Inside, she was a very big amount of embarrassed, but she couldn't help it.

"I'd much rather stay home with you, but we have a big problem at work today," Mom said.

"Izzy?" Rosa said.

Rosa came and sat on the other side of Isabel and hugged her at the same time as Mom. An Isabel sandwich! Isabel was the cheese. She was the ham. She was the lettuce.

But not the tomato.

Tomatoes = mushes.

CHEESE HAM LETTUCE

DEFINITELY NOT A DIRT SANDWICH

"Ms. Sheila?" Rosa said. "Remember that thing we talked about?"

Isabel wiped the tears off her face and listened. It must be something Very Serious, otherwise Mom would have asked Rosa just to call her Sheila, not Ms. Sheila.

"What did you talk about?" Isabel asked.

"That you're a special girl," Rosa said. "A girl with a lot of love …"

"Maybe they should make a show about me," Isabel said.

"And that maybe just your mom and me aren't enough for all that love …" Rosa said.

Mom seemed to understand what Rosa meant. It took Isabel a little longer. Two people was too small an amount for Isabel to love. So? So? So?

They needed more people!

Isabel sprang off the sofa and onto the coffee table, where she began to spin around again, shouting with happiness.

"WE'RE GETTING A BABY! WE'RE GETTING A BABY! WE'RE GETTING A BABY!"

Mom said, "No, we're not."

THE GOOD NEWS

Isabel was late for school that day. When she came in, everybody was already sitting at their tables, except for Bernadette, who stood at the front of the room getting ready to present her talent. Every Thursday was Talent Day.

Because Isabel was late, she didn't have the chance to tell Zoë, or anybody, her GOOD NEWS.

"*Psst!*" She tried a few times to get Zoë to turn around in her seat, but it was still *some of the time*. Zoë wasn't talking to her.

But Isabel was still talking to Zoë and she had GOOD NEWS.

Bernadette's talent was singing, or so she said. But when Mr. Blakie turned on the music and Bernadette began to sing, Isabel couldn't believe what a terrible singer she was. She covered her ears and started to sing quietly to herself to drown out Bernadette.

"La la la, *paloma paloma*! La la la, *paloma paloma* …"

"Is somebody else singing?" Mr. Blakie asked.

Isabel stopped. She waited with her hands over her ears until question time. Finally, the music ran out and Bernadette took a bow. Everybody had to clap.

"What a pretty song," Mr. Blakie said. "Does anybody have a question for Bernadette?"

Isabel's hand shot in the air first. Mr. Blakie said, "Isabel, is this a question or a comment?"

"It's a comment."

"Is it about Bernadette's talent?"

"Yes."

"Let's hear it then."

Isabel had wanted to tell everybody the GOOD NEWS, but now, she couldn't because it wasn't about Bernadette's talent.

"What a pretty song, Bernadette," Isabel said. "That's my comment."

"Thank you, Izzy," Bernadette said.

"I'm not finished. I also have a *suggestion*," Isabel said.

"Quickly," Mr. Blakie said. "I see other hands."

"I want to suggest a different song. It goes like this." Isabel stood up and started to sing, "La la la, *paloma paloma*! La la la, *paloma paloma* ..."

Bernadette stared at her, confused. Isabel gestured for her to sing along.

"La la la, *paloma paloma*," Bernadette sang.

Isabel sang louder, "La la la, *paloma paloma*! I have GOOD NEWS about tomorrow!"

Finally, Zoë turned her head, but only to frown at Isabel and look away again.

"You're moving?" Leon asked.

"Ha ha. Very funny, Leon. La la la, *paloma paloma*! No, I'm not moving!" Isabel sang. "Guess again!"

Bernadette stopped singing. She turned to Mr. Blakie. "Why is Isabel singing? Singing is *my* talent."

"Okay, Isabel, that's enough," Mr. Blakie said.

"La la la! I'M GETTING A DOG!"

She grinned at the back of Zoë's head.

"You're not getting a dog," Bernadette said.

"I am!" Isabel sang.

"You said you were getting a hamster and you didn't."

"I would have," sang Isabel. "But Rosa is afraid of hamsters! And mice! But she loves dogs, la la la!"

"Isabel?" Mr. Blakie said, crossing his arms. "Please continue this conversation at recess."

"It's true, la la la! You'll see on Monday!" Isabel took a bow.

THE DOG AGENCY

The next day, Friday, was makeup hooky day. Mom stayed home from work and Isabel stayed home from school. Normally, Rosa took the day off, too, but she wanted to go with them to the Dog Agency.

"Also known as the animal shelter," Mom said. She'd already bought a leash and collar.

The other different thing they did was put on clothes. Never had they gotten dressed for hooky, not even the time they ran out of milk. They just put their coats over their pajamas and went to the store. In slippers! But Mom said they would have to wear clothes now or "it wouldn't make a very good impression" — which meant they might not be accepted!

When Isabel heard this, she asked to take a bath. Because the last time she had taken a bath, she hadn't. She had run the tub, poured in a very big amount of bath salts and shampoo and bubble bath, and stirred it all up with the back scrubber like a big, stinky science experiment. Gag! Then she had pulled the plug and changed into her pajamas and not a single freckle had gotten wet.

That was one good thing about the Privacy Rule. Rosa didn't barge in on Isabel in the bathroom.

But today, she took a bath and even shampooed. Then they got in the car and drove to the Dog Agency to make a good impression. The perfumey smell in the car was coming from Isabel. She plugged her nose.

"You understand that it's not just you who gets to pick the dog, right, Izzy?" Mom said. "Rosa gets to help choose, because she'll be looking after it while you're at school and I'm at work."

Isabel unplugged her nose to answer. "Rosa wants a small dog and so do I. Right, Rosa?"

Rosa was in the passenger seat beside Mom. "Right, Izzy. "

"I want a dog that I can pretend is my baby."

"Gently," Mom said.

"Of course gently," Isabel said. "That's how you play with babies."

After that, Isabel didn't say anything, just sat breathing through her mouth. Finally,

Mom asked, "Are you okay back there?"

"I'm a small amount of nervous," Isabel admitted. What if the rubber stamp didn't come down?

They pulled up at a big, square building painted gray. Even before they went inside, they could hear the dogs barking.

The first room was an office. The woman behind the counter welcomed them, then led them down a hall. The barking got louder. She pointed to a door with a window.

"All those cats need homes, too," she said.

Isabel looked through the window. So many cats! Black cats, orange cats, tabby cats. Sleeping cats, washing cats, brother cats, sister cats, cats with no family.

Isabel started to feel funny inside,
probably because the place smelled worse
than shampoo.

They walked through a room with shelves
of cages. So many rabbits! There were
hamsters, too, running on wheels in their
cages, and a parrot. Cats, rabbits, hamsters
and a parrot with no families.

The woman opened another door and the barking got really loud. "Hey, guys and gals," she said in a cheerful voice. "We've got visitors!"

Mom and Rosa and Isabel followed her into a long room lined with bigger cages. In every cage, there was a dog without a family. Isabel closed her eyes and saw babies instead, babies in cages *wa-wa-wa*-ing and waving their arms and legs in the air. *Choose me, choose me,* they were crying. But only one would get picked.

She stuck her tongue in and out of the no-front-teeth space — poke, poke, poke — to get that feeling she liked. No good feeling came. Instead, she was a big amount of dizzy.

"Izzy?" Mom asked. "Are you okay?"

Isabel fainted. For real.

"It can be overwhelming," the shelter woman was saying when Isabel opened her eyes. She was lying on the row of chairs in the office with her head in Mom's lap.

"Hi, Izzy," Mom said. "Feel better?"

Something cold and wet was pressed into her head. Cold, wet paper towels. She didn't feel dizzy anymore, but she felt a big amount of sad.

"Do you want to go back and look at the dogs?" Mom asked.

"No," Isabel said. "Let Rosa choose."

"Okay. We'll get started on the forms."

The shelter woman handed them the

forms on a clipboard, then left to help Rosa pick a dog.

"Any dog is fine!" Isabel called after them. She sat up and said to Mom, "You didn't pick me. You just got me. Right?"

"That's right. Thank goodness. What if I'd picked somebody else?"

Izzy slumped against Mom's shoulder and watched while she wrote their names and address on the form. There were questions to answer, too. Mom read them out. "House or apartment?"

"House," Isabel said.

"Do we have a yard?"

"Yes," Isabel said.

"Why do you want a pet?"

Because I have a lot of love, Isabel was about to say. But just then, the door opened and in walked Rosa with a brown ball of fur cradled in her arms. Four legs kicked the air. Then the brown ball rolled over and looked right at Isabel.

"I LOVE HIM!" Isabel screamed.

LOVE AT FIRST SIGHT

They named him Rollo because the first thing he did was roll over. Best of all — he was an actual baby!

"I didn't know we were getting a puppy," Isabel said in the car as they drove away.

Rosa said, "I took one look at him and it was just like my show — *Love at First Sight*."

"Me, too!" Isabel said.

Rollo was sleeping in her lap now. She looked down at the little brown ball of him, closed her eyes and opened them again. Love at Second Sight! She leaned down and kissed him. She kissed him again.

"Now I know why everybody was kissing that man."

"What man?" Mom asked. She looked at Rosa.

"Sheila, I have no idea."

"The man with the big mustache in the show," Isabel said, and Mom and Rosa laughed. "His fur is so soft. I can't stop kissing him. I'm having Love at Seventh Sight now."

By the time they reached the pet store, Isabel was having Love at Thirty-Seventh Sight.

Rollo woke up when they got out of the car and — whoops! — rolled over in Isabel's arms. She nearly dropped him!

Inside, she set him on the floor. Right away, Rollo peed. Isabel was embarrassed, but the clerk came over with a roll of paper towels and a huge smile.

OH, NO!

"No worries. That's not the first puppy accident we've had here. What a cute little guy."

Isabel told the clerk everything — how she had so much love that they went to the Dog Agency. How, even though she fainted, they still accepted her. "But there was no rubber stamp!" she said.

She told him how Rosa got Love at First Sight, and then she did, and how kissing fur was so nice.

"If you like to be kissed," she told the clerk, "you should grow a mustache."

"I'm starting right this minute," he told her.

She looked down for some Love at Forty-Third Sight. "WHERE'S ROLLO!"

"Over here," Mom called. "We're shopping."

Isabel caught up to them in the cat food aisle. Rollo was running in a zigzag, bashing into everything. "Rollo? Wrong aisle. You're a dog!"

They needed so much puppy stuff that the clerk suggested the New Puppy Package: puppy-care book, bowls, a bag of food, poop bags and a squeaky banana. There was a puppy-sized collar and leash, too, that would fit him better than the one Mom had bought. All of it came in a carrying case with a handle.

"That's his crate," the clerk explained. "He'll sleep there until he's trained."

"Does he have to?" Isabel asked.

"Puppies don't wear diapers. They're crate-trained instead," the clerk said and Mom nodded.

They bought some extra things, too, like cheesy puppy treats, because the clerk said no cheese puffs for puppies.

PUPPY PACK

"We only eat cheese puffs when we play hooky," Isabel explained. "We eat them in our pajamas while watching movies."

"Nice life," the clerk said.

"Can I wrap him in a blanket? Can I pretend he's my baby?" she asked.

"He *is* your baby," he said, and Isabel thought she would faint again, but from happiness.

On the way back, they dropped Rosa off at her friend's house. When Isabel and Mom got home, Isabel wasn't allowed to bring Rollo inside until he peed.

In the backyard, Rollo had a big amount of interest in sniffing and pulling on Isabel's friendship bracelet and rolling over in the grass. He had zero interest in peeing. Isabel crawled around after him like she was the baby instead of the mother. Finally, she picked him up and carried him to the back door.

"He doesn't have to go. He went in the store, remember?"

"Then you'll have to put him in the crate," Mom called back.

So Isabel decided to play with her baby outside. She got down on her knees and gently lifted Rollo into her lap.

"AHHH!"

She leapt up with Rollo and ran into the house. "Mom! He peed! He peed on *me*!"

Mom took Rollo from her. She was laughing. "I can't count the number of times you peed on me."

"No way!" Isabel said.

"Go change. Now you can play with him inside. Gently."

Just then, the phone rang. Rollo's floppy ears perked up and he began to bark his head off at the phone. *Yip, yip, yip! Yip, yip, yip!* His squeaky voice didn't match his fierce expression. It was so funny that Isabel and Mom buckled over laughing. Rollo only stopped barking when Isabel answered the phone.

YIP!
GRRR YIP!
YIP! GRRR
YIP!

BRRRING
BRRRING
BRRRING

It was Grandma calling to ask about
the new member of the family. Isabel went
upstairs to change and took the phone so she
could tell her about the Dog Agency and the
pet store and Love at First Sight.

"Grandma, he's the cutest, funniest puppy
you ever saw. But he's scared of the phone!"
Then she asked, "Is it true I peed on Mom?"

Grandma said yes!

By the time Isabel finished talking and
came back downstairs in her hooky pajamas,
Rollo was in the crate. He'd fallen asleep in
Mom's arms.

Isabel slumped. "Again?"

It was lunchtime anyway, so Isabel brought
the crate to the table and set it on a chair.

Mom said no.

"Why not?"

"Rollo isn't going to sit at the table with us, even when he's house trained," Mom said.

"Why?" Isabel asked.

"Because he's a dog."

"Why can't dogs eat at the table?"

Mom made the same teeny mouth as Zoë, though on Mom, it didn't mean she was mad. It meant that she would only answer two "why" questions in a row. Isabel could ask as many as she wanted. She could fall down the Why Hole and never climb back out if she wanted, but Mom wouldn't fall down with her.

"Under the table?"

Mom nodded. Isabel slid the crate under

the table and sat down to eat. "What's the reason Rollo can't sleep in a crib like a real baby," she asked. "Notice I didn't say *why*?"

"According to the puppy book," Mom said, "puppies like crates. They like them because when dogs were wild, they lived in caves."

"So Rollo thinks the crate is a cave and he's wild?"

"Yes."

WILD ROLLO

Isabel looked under the table at the plastic crate. Under the table was like a cave, too. She slithered off her chair. "Mom! I'm in a cave! Can you pass me my sandwich?"

Mom let Isabel eat lunch in the cave with Rollo. When Isabel barked, Mom nudged a plate of apple slices into the cave.

After she finished eating, it was a big amount of boring just sitting in a cave waiting for Rollo to wake up.

"You know, Mom? When they find out at school that I really did get a dog, everybody's going to want to come over for a play date. So while Rollo's sleeping, we should make cupcakes. Because Monday's going to be a party."

Mom was loading the dishwasher. She said, "One friend at a time. You don't want to overwhelm Rollo."

"Do puppies faint?"

"Probably. And you don't want to overwhelm Rosa either."

"Right." She crawled out from under the table. "Mom? With so many play dates, I'll never be alone while Rosa is watching her show. Even when Zoë's mad at me because I keep getting her in trouble."

"You do?" Mom asked.

"Yes. I was in the doghouse because of it. But now we're *all* in the doghouse — because a dog lives here!"

She just had to shout it. "What a nice life!"

Isabel thought of something else, then. "Mom? If I'm going to have a play date every day, who should I choose after Zoë?"

"Do what I do at work. Make a schedule."

Isabel ran off to get paper and her pencil case.

Back in the kitchen, she checked on Rollo in the cave. Sleeping. Then she sat down to make the schedule. Mom showed her one on the computer. Isabel copied the days of the week and drew the lines for the names.

She checked on Rollo. Sleeping.

The schedule looked too plain. She decorated it with little drawings of squeaky bananas and poop bags.

"What's a squeaky banana for?" she asked.

Mom was across the table from Isabel,

drinking coffee and working on her computer. She said, "It's just a dog toy."

"Do dogs eat bananas?" Isabel asked. Before Mom could answer, she thought of an even more interesting question.

"What if bananas really squeaked?"

Mom kept her eyes on the computer screen.

"Maybe they do squeak, but we just can't hear them. What would bananas talk about? Mom?"

"Those are the kinds of questions you might wonder about, but not ask," Mom told her.

"Okay," she said. "I'll wonder about them while I work on the schedule. But first, I'll check on my baby."

Sleeping!

She filled all the names in, even Leon's. There were still spaces, so she wrote some names more than once.

Zoë.

Zoë.

Zoë.

Mom got up from the table with her coffee and took it to the microwave to warm it up. When the microwave started beeping, a growl came from under the table. Then *yip, yip, yip! Yip, yip, yip!*

Isabel opened the crate. Her ferocious baby came charging out, barking and leaping at the microwave until the beeping stopped and he fell onto his bum. Isabel fell onto her bum, too, laughing instead of barking.

DO NOT USE

That evening, Isabel was a very big amount
of tired, too tired to bake cupcakes. Too tired
to watch a hooky movie and eat cheese puffs.
Too tired from looking after her baby and all
the exercise she got taking him outside and
bringing him back in.

Only once did she get to wrap him in a blanket and lift him gently onto her lap. But he rolled right over and set off exploring the house. Isabel had to follow him because you can't leave a baby alone ever, not even for a second. Something terrible could happen.

For example: the baby could start chewing on electrical cords, which was Very Dangerous. Or the baby could bash into a plant stand and knock it over, which was Very Messy. Or the baby could squeeze his head under the bookshelf and get stuck with just his tail and back legs sticking out, which was Very Scary for his mother and for the baby, who was crying, *Yip, yip, yip!*

When that Very Scary thing happened, Isabel ran for the squeaky banana. But Rollo was just a baby. He didn't know to be surprised that a banana was talking to him. He couldn't understand that the squeaky banana was saying, "Back out, Rollo." So Isabel tried to pry Rollo out from under the bookshelf — gently! — using the squeaky banana.

Finally, Rollo figured out how to flatten himself and turn in a circle and wriggle out. Then he had an accident on the white carpet, also Very Messy.

Anytime the phone rang, or the microwave beeped, Rollo would come running from wherever he was to yip at it. Once, he was at the top of the stairs when Rosa turned the microwave on, which was Very Dangerous *and* Very Scary, so Isabel made a DO NOT USE sign and taped it to the microwave. Mom said they couldn't turn the ringer off the phone because then they wouldn't know if somebody was calling.

At the end of the day, after Rollo fell asleep, Isabel dragged herself upstairs, brushed her teeth and went to bed.

Mom came to say goodnight. "Now you're learning. Sleep when the baby sleeps. That was the best advice I got."

"Can the crate be in my room?" Isabel asked.

"I don't think that's a good idea," Mom said. "If he wakes in the night, you'll have to wake up, too. He's better off in my room."

"I want to! *Please?*"

"Okay. Just tonight."

Mom brought the crate and set it by Isabel's bed. She also brought a flashlight.

The second Mom left the room, Isabel got up, opened the crate and lifted Rollo out.

Asleep, he was floppy, like a stuffed dog, not a real one. She climbed back into bed and — finally! finally! — cuddled her new baby in her arms.

"La la la, *paloma, paloma,*" she sang.

Before long, she was asleep, too.

Then the light snapped on. Isabel sat up, blinking with surprise. There was Mom, standing over her, looking a very big amount of annoyed.

"Isabel. Rollo has to sleep in the crate."

"Okay," Isabel said.

She slid out of bed, kissed Rollo and shut him in the crate. Mom picked up the crate by the handle.

"No! Please! Don't take away the crate. I

won't take him out again. I promise. Only if
he wakes up."

Mom heaved a big sigh and set down the
crate. Then she said, "After this long day,
I could use a snuggle
with *my* baby, too."
Isabel smiled
and threw the
covers back
for Mom
to get in.

"Mom? When you first saw me, did you have Love at First Sight?" Isabel asked.

"You'd better believe it."

"Was it hard looking after me?"

Mom laughed. "You'd better believe that, too. I was overwhelmed. If it wasn't for Rosa, I don't know what I would have done. Babies are small, but they sure take it out of you."

Isabel said, "I'm sorry I peed on you."

Mom laughed again and hugged Isabel goodnight.

As soon as Mom left, Isabel got out of bed. She arranged the pillows and cushions on the floor, pulled down the blankets and scooched right up against the hard plastic of the crate.

She was a very small amount of comfortable,
but she fell right to sleep.

THE BLABS!

All weekend, Isabel looked after Rollo.
She took him outside and brought him
back in. She lifted him up to the phone so
he could sniff it and not be afraid. She did
such a good job being Rollo's mother that
Mom let her keep the crate in her room
every night.

Isabel was an even bigger amount of tired
on Monday morning from all that Rollo
exercise and not sleeping when the baby
slept. She would have asked to stay home
except that she remembered the schedule.

She took it off the fridge and reread it while she crunched four times through her cereal.

Rosa told her, "You're going to be a popular girl, Izzy."

"I know. Nobody believed I was getting a dog. But let's not bring Rollo with us this morning. I want to keep him a surprise until after school."

"Sure," Rosa said.

"I just hope I don't blab."

"It's going to be a hard day for you," Rosa said.

It was going to be hardest not to blab to Zoë. For once, it would be good if it was still *some of the time*!

Isabel decided to practice *not* blabbing on the way to school. She told Rosa, "I won't say one thing about Rollo. Pretend you're Zoë. Ask about my weekend."

"How was your weekend?" Rosa asked.

THESE BLAB-PROOFING METHODS ARE <u>NOT</u> RECOMMENDED.

"Fine, la la la," Isabel said.

"Anything special happen?"

"Nope, la la la."

"Are those funny red speckles on your nose from a dog chewing your face?"

"What speckles?" Isabel touched her nose. "Oops. I mean, what dog?"

They got all the way to school without any blabbing. Then, when Rosa hugged her goodbye, Isabel said, "Don't forget the schedule when you bring Rollo to pick me up."

"Gotcha!" Rosa crowed.

"That doesn't count!"

"Okay, okay," Rosa said as she walked away. "Good luck, Izzy."

"Thanks! I'm going to need it!"

Did she ever! The first person she saw when she got to her cubby was Zoë. The first person on the schedule. Isabel had to make a tight line with her mouth and turn her head away as she hung up her coat.

Zoë said, "Look, Izzy. My coat is holding hands with your coat again. I'm not mad anymore. Do you want to have a play date at my house today?"

"Maybe you'll want to come to my house instead," Isabel told her. "But don't ask me why because I can't tell you. I can only say that your name is first on the schedule."

"What schedule?" Zoë said.

The blabs! Isabel clamped her hand over her mouth and ran to her table without answering. She kept her head down and wouldn't look at Zoë, the same way Zoë wouldn't look at Isabel *some of the time*.

All through Show and Tell, Isabel sat with her elbows on the table and both hands over her mouth to hold in the blabs.

Paul C. was presenting his Show and Tell. Math was his hobby. He stood at the front of the class and showed them the workbooks he'd finished for fun. Mr. Blakie asked him to count them. Then he got him to make stacks.

"If there are five workbooks in this pile, and Paul moves three workbooks to this pile …"

Normally, Isabel's hand would shoot in the air so that she could tell everybody that Mr. Blakie was sneaking in math. But not today. Today, if she took her hands off her mouth, she'd blab for sure. Instead, she sat propped up on her elbows. Behind her hands, she yawned.

Paul C. finished. Normally, Isabel would raise her hand in the air for question time, too, even before she'd thought of a question.

"Isabel? Don't you have a question for Paul?" Mr. Blakie asked.

Isabel shook her head. Behind her hands, she yawned again.

Zoë said, "Mr. Blakie? Something's the matter with Isabel. She hasn't said anything for fifteen minutes."

Patty said, "Izzy? Are you okay?"

"She's not going to throw up, is she?"
Leon asked. "She's holding her hands over
her mouth."

Mr. Blakie got everybody busy with seat
work. Then he came over to Isabel and
crouched down. "Do you feel sick, Isabel?"

If she *was* sick, Mr. Blakie would send her
to the nurse's room, where she wouldn't have
anybody to blab to.

She nodded. Mr. Blakie put one hand
around her shoulder and guided her out of
her seat and over to the door. He picked up
the garbage can with his other hand and told
the class he'd be back in a minute.

Isabel smiled at everybody behind her
hands. Worried eyes looked back.

Mr. Blakie and Isabel and the garbage can started down the hall. It wasn't until they reached the sickroom that Isabel realized Mr. Blakie had brought the garbage can in case Isabel threw up on the way. She squeezed her mouth so she couldn't laugh.

She lay down on the sickroom cot. Mr. Blakie covered her with the cozy blanket. "The nurse will be here soon. Hang in there, Isabel."

Isabel nodded in a slow, sick way. Only when Mr. Blakie closed the door did she take her hands off her mouth and relax. As soon as she relaxed, she fell asleep.

The sound of the bell woke her. The nurse was smiling down on her. Isabel sat up. "Was that the recess bell?"

"It was the lunch bell," the nurse said. "You've been sleeping your head off. How do you feel?"

"I FEEL SO HAPPY!" Isabel shouted. Then she blabbed. She couldn't hold it in a second longer.

"The only thing the matter with me is that I have TOO MUCH LOVE. But now, I have a dog. He's my very own baby and he's called

Rollo because he rolls over so much. We adopted him on Friday. I wish we'd got him diapers, too. I wouldn't be so tired if we did."

"So you're not sick?" the nurse asked.

"No. Please don't send me home. I want to surprise everybody after school. Nobody believed that I was getting a dog, but I did. I'm going to show them. I MADE A SCHEDULE!"

WOULD YOU LIKE ME TO ADD YOU TO THE SCHEDULE? NEXT TUESDAY IS FREE!

"I certainly won't send you home if you're not sick. But I have to send you back to your classroom."

"But what if I blab?" Isabel thought of something then. "Do you have any Band-Aids?"

"Of course. This is the sickroom."

Just then, Mrs. Kinoshita's voice came on the intercom. "Will the nurse please report to the basketball court?"

The nurse opened a cupboard and took out a box of Band-Aids.

"I can do it," Isabel told her.

"You sure?"

"I'm sure."

"Okay. I have to check out a situation."

After the nurse left, Isabel turned over
the empty garbage can and stood on it so she
could look at herself in the sickroom mirror.
Wow! Freckles, freckles, freckles.

When Isabel showed up in the classroom
with six Band-Aids holding her mouth closed,
everybody started laughing. Mr. Blakie made
her remove them because it was Distracting.

Luckily, she'd already told the nurse about
Rollo, so it was a bit easier to hold in the blabs.

ROLLO DOING WHAT HE DOES BEST.

YIP, YIP, RING, BEEP, BEEP

The end-of-school bell rang — finally! — and Isabel bolted out the door without even stopping at her cubby.

Zoë called after her, "Izzy? Am I still coming to your house?"

"Yes!" Isabel shouted back. "I'll see you outside!"

She ran all the way to the main door. There was Rosa with Rollo chewing on his leash, pulling on it, tying Rosa up with it.

Isabel had lost count of how much she loved him. She raced down the steps and sank onto all fours. Rollo washed her face with kisses. She scooped him up and waited for everybody else.

The first kids to pour out the door were from other classes. As soon as they saw Rollo, they gathered around. Before long, a big crowd had formed. Isabel kept her eye on the door.

At last, the kids from her class began to come out — Zoë and Bernadette and Nima, followed by Leon, Ori and Paul C. They saw Isabel holding Rollo surrounded by half the school.

"GOTCHA!!!" Isabel shouted.

The whole class pushed through the crowd to get closer. They believed her now!

"Awwww!"

"He's so so so so cute!"

"Can I pat him?"

"What's his name?"

"When did you get him?"

"Can we have a play date?"

"Yes!" Isabel said and she waved Rosa over. Rosa had the schedule. Isabel passed it around. "It has to be one at a time or Rollo will get overwhelmed."

"Look! I'm first!" Zoë said.

"Ask your dad," Isabel told her. "Then we have to go. It's almost time for Rosa's show."

To everybody else, she said, "Bye! See you tomorrow!"

On the way home, Zoë said, "Thank you for choosing me first, Izzy. Rollo's so so so so so cute!"

"Of course you're first."

She started telling Zoë about the Dog Agency. "We weren't even going to get a puppy. Just a small dog. Remember how

we played babies with those boys and mine
wouldn't be a proper baby? Now I have one!"

SHOW THAT
BUTTERFLY WHO'S
THE BOSS,
ROLLO!

RUFF!

"Can I hold the leash?" Zoë asked.

Isabel handed it to Zoë. Rollo grabbed it in
his teeth and tugged.

"I fainted while we were at the Agency."

Rollo ran around Zoë, play-growling. She had to turn a circle to free herself from the leash.

"Do you want to play babies with Rollo?" Isabel asked.

"I just love his pink tongue," Zoë said.

"It's a lot of work. I mean, a lot! He chews electrical cords."

"His waggy tail is so cute."

Rosa said, "Izzy, I don't think she's listening."

"She has Love at First Sight," Isabel said.

Rollo stopped pulling and peed. "Good Rollo!" Isabel cried. "Now we can play inside with him."

But by the time they got home, Rollo was tired from the long walk to school and back. When Isabel set him on the floor, he marched

right over to his crate and curled up inside
it. They heard a big Rollo sigh. His sighs
were bigger than him. The puppy book said
a sigh meant contentment, which was like
happiness, but calmer.

"He thinks that's his cave," Isabel explained.

SOOOO CUTE!

Both girls lay on their stomachs on the
floor so they could pat and scratch Rollo
inside the crate. In a few minutes, his eyes
closed. Isabel sat up and shut the door.

"How long is he going to sleep?" Zoë asked.

"I'm not sure. I'll show you his puppy stuff."

Mom had put all of Rollo's things in a basket. Isabel took it from the cupboard and showed Zoë his brush and ball, his cheesy treats and toys. Isabel squeaked the banana, then Zoë did.

After that, they checked the crate. Rollo was still sleeping.

Then Zoë got an idea. "Let's play puppies."

"Good idea," Isabel said. "We can make a Dog Agency."

They took the basket upstairs to Isabel's room. The stuffed toys were crammed in the bookcase. Isabel and Zoë arranged them on the furniture and the floor.

"Were there bears and rabbits at the Dog Agency?" Zoë asked.

"There were rabbits."

Zoë said, "Okay. You be the puppy first."

That wasn't how Isabel thought they were going to play. She didn't want to be a sad dog without a family. "The toys are the puppies. We'll come and adopt them."

"Toys can't do anything," Zoë said. "You be the puppy first. Then I will."

Isabel felt better knowing they were taking turns. She got down on her hands and knees.

"Don't forget to bark," Zoë told her. She went out and closed the door behind her.

Isabel barked a few times. Zoë came back in. "Look at all these cute animals!" she exclaimed. "Which one will I pick? This one? Or this one?"

Zoë walked slowly around the room. Isabel barked more frantically, like Rollo with the microwave, trying to get Zoë to pick her. She rolled over and kicked her legs in the air the way Rollo did. She sat up again and panted enthusiastically with her tongue out.

"This dog is cute," Zoë said, peering down at Isabel.

Isabel jumped up and licked Zoë's face.

"Yuck!" Zoë screeched.

EWWWW.!

"I did that because I love you," Isabel said.
"That's how puppies kiss."

"But puppies don't talk." Zoë wiped the
place Isabel licked, then wiped the lick on
Isabel's shirt.

"Ew," Isabel said.

First, they were playing puppies, then
they were passing a lick back and forth and

laughing their heads off. Already they were having a big amount of fun.

"Okay, let's keep playing," Zoë said when they finally calmed down. She put on a serious face and turned a circle, taking one last look at all the toys. "It's so hard to choose!"

"Pick me! Pick me!" Isabel barked.

Zoë pointed to a stuffed bear. "This is the one I want."

"Hey!" Isabel said. "What about me?"

Zoë started to leave with the bear. "Maybe if you don't lick people, you'll get picked sooner."

Isabel called after her, "And maybe that bear will eat you!"

Zoë dropped the bear and ran back to Isabel. "I changed my mind."

Both of them started laughing again. Zoë took the leash out of the basket and clipped it to the neck of Isabel's shirt. She led her out of the Agency with the basket under her arm.

Isabel was feeling hungry by then from rolling around and jumping up and trying to get Zoë to pick her. "Let's go get a sna—"

Zoë cut her off. "No talking, remember?"

Right. How did Rollo show he was hungry? Isabel was on her hands and knees crawling past the hall table. Under it, she saw the lamp plugged into the wall. Hungry puppies chew, but chewing cords was Very Dangerous. Unless she unplugged the lamp. Then it would be Very Funny!

Isabel crawled under the table, unplugged the lamp and started gumming the cord.

Zoë peered under the table. "What are you doing?"

"Yum. A lamp cord," Isabel said, even though she wasn't supposed to talk.

This was just about the funniest thing Zoë had ever heard. She laughed so hard she had to run to the bathroom. When she came back, she brought a long strip of toilet paper, which she tucked into the back of Isabel's skirt.

"That's your tail. Now, chew this instead, you bad little puppy."

Zoë took the squeaky banana out of the basket and put it in Isabel's mouth. It tasted like yucky plastic. No wonder Rollo didn't want to chew it. Dirt tasted better than that banana!

They went downstairs, Isabel with the toilet-paper tail dragging behind her and the plastic banana in her mouth. It wasn't easy crawling headfirst down the stairs. Rollo was actually too small to do it, but Isabel didn't say this because she wasn't supposed to talk. Also, she couldn't with a plastic banana in her mouth.

At the bottom of the stairs, Zoë said, "Oops! I stepped on your tail and ripped it in half."

What a terrible mother, Isabel wanted to say. It was so hard being a puppy!

They headed past the living room, where Rosa was watching her show, to the kitchen, where, to Isabel's surprise, a plate of chimichangas was sitting on the counter. Rosa must have set them out while Izzy and Zoë were upstairs.

She sat on her haunches and let the squeaky banana fall to the floor. Hungrily, she stuck out her tongue.

Zoë picked up a chimichanga. "What is this?"

Only Isabel's favorite after-school snack and her second-favorite word after *accepted*!

Zoë sniffed it. "Smells yummy …"

It smelled delicious! Outside it was crunchy, but the spicy inside was soft. Rosa's chimichangas never, ever got the mushes. The soft middle never ruined the crunch. It was magic. Not even Rosa knew why.

Isabel barked. She was drooling like a
real dog.

Zoë took a bite. "Yum!"

Isabel barked again and pawed at Zoë. She
stretched herself up so that Zoë would give
her a bite.

"Are you hungry, too, little puppy?" Zoë said, eating the rest of the chimichanga. "Here. Let me give you something to eat."

She'd set the basket on the table. Now, she took out the package of dog treats and, giggling, shook a few out on the floor. Isabel bent her head and sniffed the treats. Instead of a nice cheesy smell, she smelled nothing. Did they taste like nothing, too?

Poor Rollo! If they didn't taste good, Isabel would throw them out.

"I'm only joking," Zoë said. "You can have a chimi-thingie."

Isabel bowed tongue-first over the treats on the floor.

"Izzy, don't *really* eat them!" Zoë said.

With the tip of her tongue, Isabel touched one. Sure enough, they were nothing-flavored treats.

"YUCK!!!" Zoë screamed.

"Shhh!" Isabel told her. "You'll wake Rollo."

She turned to look at the crate in the corner. "Rollo?"

The door was wide open! Isabel leapt up and hurried over to the crate.

Zoë followed. "He's not there. How did he get out?"

"Maybe I forgot to latch it."

"Where do you think he went?" Zoë asked.

"Maybe Rosa has him. I'll check. You stay here.

Isabel crept to the
living room and peeked
in the door. Rosa was
staring at the TV. In her lap was a square blue
tissue box, not a small brown ball of fur.

Isabel hurried back to the kitchen.

"Zoë, we have to find him. You can't leave
a baby alone ever, not even for a second.
Something terrible could happen."

Zoë's eyes got wide. "What? What could
happen? What? What? What?"

"He could chew cords that aren't unplugged or get stuck under something. Or knock something over and get squashed."

Isabel started calling, "Rollo! Here, Rollo!"

He had to be in another room doing something Very Dangerous or Very Scary or Very Messy. Isabel hoped it was just something Very Messy, like yesterday, when he got into the bathroom and scattered dirty tissues from the wastebasket all around.

They rushed to the bathroom. No Rollo. The dictionary was still weighing down the wastebasket lid.

HOW DO YOU SPELL
UHOHSTARTING TO FEEL A BIT PANICKYNOW?

They checked Mom's office, where the day before yesterday, Rollo had knocked over the paper shredder and rolled around in the mess and came out looking like he had a very bad case of puppy dandruff.

No Rollo.

"Where are you, Rollo?" Isabel called in a quavery voice.

"Upstairs?" Zoë said.

"He can't climb the stairs."

Isabel sank onto the floor and closed her eyes. They were having a big amount of scary no-fun now. "Maybe he's stuck somewhere. Maybe he's answering us but we can't hear him."

They stopped talking and listened very

hard. Isabel heard birds outside and cars driving past and, from the kitchen, the purring of the fridge. She heard Spanish voices talking on the TV and violins.

Finally, Isabel said, "Let's get Rosa."

They ran and burst into the living room, making Rosa jump about three feet in the air. "*¿Qué está pasando, Izzy?*"

"Rollo's gone!" both girls cried.

Rosa got up right away. "Did you check the bathroom?"

"Yes."

"Your mom's office?"

"We checked everywhere!" Isabel said.

"But not upstairs," Zoë said.

"Maybe he somehow got up there. You'd better look," Rosa said.

"I'll check the backyard."

Isabel and Zoë searched both the upstairs bedrooms, in and under the beds, and in the closets, too. They checked the bathroom. No Rollo. Isabel closed her eyes again. She stuck her tongue in and out of the no-front-teeth space to help her think. Zoë didn't say "yuck."

"What would your mom do if she lost you?" Isabel asked Zoë.

"She'd call the police!"

"That's it!" she told Zoë. Instead of running down the stairs, Isabel jumped onto the banister and slid all the way down.

Rosa was just coming in from outside. "We're calling the police!" Zoë told her.

"No," Isabel said. "We're calling ourselves."

"Huh?" Zoë said.

Isabel picked the plate of chimichangas off the counter and handed them to Rosa.

Rosa knew just what to do. She tore the DO NOT USE sign off the microwave, slid the plate inside and turned it on. From her back pocket, she whipped out her phone and speed-dialed. At exactly the same moment, the ringing and beeping started.

And out of nowhere came a ferocious yipping puppy. First he growled and barked at the beeping microwave, then he raced over to growl and bark at the ringing phone, back and forth, back and forth — *yip, yip, ring, beep, yip, yip, ring, beep* — until he got so dizzy he tumbled right onto his bum.

NICE LIFE

"I was so scared for Rollo," Zoë said. "Where do you think he was?"

Rosa and Isabel were walking her home, Isabel and Zoë holding the leash together, their hands close so their matted gray-and-beige friendship bracelets could be together, too.

Isabel shrugged. "*Yip, yip, ring, beep!*" she sang. "*Yip, yip, ring, beep!* That's my second-favorite song after Rosa's *paloma* song."

"*Yip, yip, ring, beep!*" Zoë sang along until both of them were laughing too hard to sing.

DOES THIS LOOK LIKE A DOG WHO GOT AWAY WITH SOMETHING? DEFINITELY YES.

Rollo had no idea how much trouble he'd caused. He zigzagged happily, pulling on his leash, then stopping to sniff — the grass, a tree, the fire hydrant.

When they got to Zoë's house, the two girls hugged goodbye. Zoë said, "You were right, Izzy. A puppy really is a lot of work. But he's so much fun! I love him, and I love you!"

"Bye! I love you, too!" Isabel called back.

Isabel slumped against Rosa then. "A puppy's a lot of work, but *being one* is so much harder! I'm starving and I bet Rollo is, too."

"Those chimichangas are waiting for you," Rosa said.

They started walking home, Isabel holding hands with Rosa, her other hand holding the leash.

Poor Rollo! All that was waiting for him were nothing-flavored treats.

Isabel squeezed Rosa's hand. *"Pleeeeeeeeease, Rosa, can Rollo have a chimichanga, too?"*

That night, Isabel heard a whimpering sound. She heard it in her dream, the dream where she lived in a doghouse with the sweetest puppy all shaggy and brown. In the dream, he kept rolling over so they called him ...

"Rollo!"

Isabel sat up. It was the middle of the night. She could tell because the room was so dark. When she turned on the light, she saw a little brown face peeking out of the grate on the door of the crate.

"Hold on, Rollo." She grabbed the flashlight.

All the way down the stairs, Rollo squirmed under her arm. She ran for the back door.

"Way to go, Rollo! I'm still dry."

Outside, she set him gently on the grass and shone the flashlight for him. He bumbled off in a zigzag, lost his balance and tipped over. Then, since he was already down, why not roll over? He found a stick and began to chew it.

Isabel yawned. "Did you go? Can we go back to bed?"

She looked up at the sky. The stars were sprayed out above her. Sky freckles!

"Finished, Rollo?"

She sat down. Rollo came running over and grabbed her pajama cuff. He tugged,

making funny little growls. She flopped
onto her back, and he climbed on her
chest and began to lick her face and chew
her nose.

"You crazy baby!"
Isabel laughed.

"Izzy?" she heard. "Are you out here?"
"Yes!"
Mom looked like a ghost in her white
pajamas, walking across the lawn. She sat
next to Isabel. "You scared me. I heard a

noise and I went to check on you, but you were gone."

"Here we are," Isabel said.

"Yes. Here we are."

Mom lay down next to Isabel in the grass. Rollo climbed up on her now and licked her face, too, and chewed her nose. They scooched closer to keep warm. For a long time, they just stared up at the beautiful star-freckled sky.

Rollo sighed, then Isabel did.

"Nice life," she said.

IZZY AND ROLLO SANDWICH

CAROLINE ADDERSON is the acclaimed, award-winning author of the Jasper John Dooley series, as well as many other books for readers of all ages. Caroline lives in Vancouver, British Columbia, with her husband and her tree-climbing Jack Russell terrier, Mickey.

KELLY COLLIER is the author-illustrator of *A Horse Named Steve* and *Team Steve*. She has an identical twin sister who is her best friend (most of the time) and her favorite person (all of the time). Kelly lives in Toronto, Ontario, with her husband and their dog.

HELLO? ARE YOU STILL THERE?

INCOMING!

MORE IZZY BOOKS

AVAILABLE SOON!